WORLDS OF IMAGINATION

Edited By Kelly Reeves

First published in Great Britain in 2020 by:

Young Writers
Remus House
Coltsfoot Drive
Peterborough
PE2 9BF
Telephone: 01733 890066
Website: www.youngwriters.co.uk

Printed and bound in the UK by BookPrintingUK
Website: www.bookprintinguk.com
YB0438T

FOREWORD

Welcome, Reader!

Are you ready to enter the Adventure Zone? Then come right this way - your portal to endless new worlds awaits. It's very simple, all you have to do is turn the page and you'll be transported into a wealth of super stories.

Is it magic? Is it a trick? No! It's all down to the skill and imagination of primary school pupils from around the country. We gave them the task of writing a story on any topic, and to do it in just 100 words! I think you'll agree they've achieved that brilliantly – this book is jam-packed with exciting and thrilling tales.

These young authors have brought their ideas to life using only their words. This is the power of creativity and it gives us life too! Here at Young Writers we want to pass our love of the written word onto the next generation and what better way to do that than to celebrate their writing by publishing it in a book!

It sets their work free from homework books and notepads and puts it where it deserves to be – out in the world and preserved forever. Each awesome author in this book should be **super proud** of themselves, and now they've got proof of their ideas and their creativity in black and white, to look back on in years to come!

We hope you enjoy this book as much as we have. Now it's time to let imagination take control, so read on...

CONTENTS

Scarlet Dalton (10) 53
Edward Palmer (9) 54
Louis Nthakomwa-Cassidy (8) 55
Toyel Tojo (10) 56
Theo James Brown (11) 57
Aimee Richards (10) 58
Neve Pritchard-Doughty (9) 59
Ellie Zulerons (10) 60
Joash Sam Samuel (10) 61
Jaydan James Whitmore (10) 62
Grace Amelia Bryning (10) 63
Josh Marvell (10) 64
Maxwell Cheung-Ross (10) 65
Karin Karzan Karim (11) 66
Maisy Dalton (10) 67
Emily Dilkes (9) 68
Ava Francess Brown (9) 69
Karishma Garratt (8) 70
Miller Sweet (10) 71
Lena Maria Pigan (10) 72
Terrence Vooi (8) 73
Jack Griffin (11) 74
Yasmine Bhihe (10) 75
Jack Newton (10) 76
Poppy Sone (10) 77
Paige Tebbutt (10) 78

Grange Park Primary School, Winchmore Hill

Aslı Çetin (9) 79
Christiana Maria Christofi (9) 80
Harry Stylianou (9) 81
Jacob Polak (10) 82
Reggie Perkins 83
Daria Valizadeh (10) 84
Amelia Marrison-Claffey (9) 85
Nihar Vaidya (9) 86
Anastasi Kyriacou (10) 87
Antonia Charalambous (10) 88
Jing-Yang Koh (9) 89
Nadeem Ezzedine (9) 90
Amelie Hon (9) 91
Omotobi Olulode (9) 92
Kemal Yilmaz (9) 93
Emmerson Camp (10) 94
Talia Penn (9) 95
Jeyda Dervish (9) 96
Havin Uludag (9) 97
Ollie Tini (10) 98

Greenhill Academy, Glodwick

Haleemah Ali (9) 99
Inaya Chowdury (7) 100
Somaya Iqbal (7) 101
Shuaib Hussain (9) 102
Khadija Rahman (7) 103
Anabia Kawal (10) 104
Maya Choudhury (9) 105
Halima Sadia (9) 106
Muhammed Ali 107
Muhammad Yahya Khan (8) 108
Saffa Fatima (8) 109

Janet Duke Primary School, Laindon

Beatrice Olafusi (10) 110
Darcey Elizabeth Wealthall (10) 111
Katy-Rose Edwards (10) 112
Rose Ever Ikpeba (11) 113
Chloe Tilley (10) 114

Larkfield Primary School, Southport

Maisie Grace Midgley (9) 115
Matthew Hand (10) 116
Theo Johnson (9) 117
Rose Jackson (7) 118
Lucy Jolly (8) 119
Harriet Smith (9) & Amelia Selby (10) 120
Heidi Mabel Sunners (9) 121
Isabella Huang (7) 122
Evie Lavery (9) 123

Park Wood Schools Federation, Rainham

Holly Millward (8)	124
Grace Burberry (7)	125
Mia Becconsall (8)	126
Emmie Faith Walker (8)	127
Emilia Payne (7)	128
Jessie Gore (7)	129
Savannah Morrison (8)	130
Ronin (7)	131
Oliver Wood (8)	132
Ethan Newman (7)	133
Zack Andrew Gibbs (7)	134
Freya Hatton (7)	135
Molly Swanson Kirwan (7)	136
Libby Paternoster (7)	137
Jack Paul Tandy (8)	138
Grace Bevis (8)	139
Harrison Pope (7)	140
Myah Flemming (7)	141
Selyena Sekmen (7)	142
Isla-Rose Vernon (8)	143
Brooke Lenihan (8)	144
Heidi Ongley (8)	145
Finley Bunting (7)	146
Thomas Harrison-Brookes (8)	147

Pelsall Village School, Pelsall

April Charmaine Freeman (10), Lemie Francis (11) & Layla	148
Lemie Francis (10)	149
Lilli-Mai Smith (10)	150
Bethlyn Rose Brotherton (11)	151

Stella Maris School, Heaton Mersey

Sonny Lindley (10)	152
Bradley Beckford	153
Lily (8)	154
Agatha Charlotte Hayes (9)	155
Osikhena Otu (10)	156

Zak Shahid (10)	157
Max Edgar (8)	158
Zoha Mahmood (8)	159
Oscar Hargreaves	160
William Taylor (8)	161
Lily Richardson-Gormley (8)	162
Rose Ameerah Khan (8)	163
Megan Carter-Jones	164
Cara Taylor	165
Hadi Ejaz (11)	166
Eva Cunningham (8)	167
Lily-Mae Bullas (9)	168
Eason Fong (10)	169

THE STORIES

TOP SECRET

The New And Advanced World

"Maya, could you get me some decorations from the basement?" said Mum.

"Sure, Mum!" said Maya.

She gracefully went down the basement stairs and found a bright, big time portal.

"Wow!" Maya exclaimed. "I really want to go inside."

Maya slowly stepped forward and it swallowed her whole. To her surprise, she saw flying cars, talking animals, flying shoes, planes as fast as lightning and much more.

She approached a lady and said, "What year is this?"

"2055," she said awkwardly.

This could possibly mean one thing, Maya was in our new, advanced and amazing world.

Jameelah Opeloyeru (10)
Allen Edwards Primary School, Stockwell

A Bunch Of Things That'll Blow Your Mind

I'm going to tell you something that'll blow your mind. If your brain explodes, I'm really sorry. I live in a parallel dimension to yours, where things like sickness and poverty don't exist! Pretty good, huh? Anyway, in my universe, the Earth, well... turned radioactive! So scary, but cool! Ever heard of global warming? This is what happened in my world but we survived. All that energy obliterated the space-time continuum and now we can time travel! But your Earth is different. It will be destroyed. So please, save the planet or both universes will be destroyed because they're parallel!

Nabil Eddahabi (10)
Allen Edwards Primary School, Stockwell

The Theft Story

You have been selected for a special top-secret assignment. Should you choose to accept to join the Julienne Sills Birthday Mission, you'll be travelling incognito on a bus to the International Spy Museum in Washington DC. Once you arrive, you will be briefed as to the nature of the international mission. You will have more fun than you can imagine, but be prepared... comfortable shoes are a must! Don't share the information with anybody because this is top-secret! Also, someone else stole £250,000 from Barclays bank, 2012. Mission details: Sunday, February 14th, 2012. Time: 10.20am sharp.

Taejon Dowdie (10)
Allen Edwards Primary School, Stockwell

The Not-So-Happy Ending Quest

It was a breezy spring Friday when me, Kayla, Leia, Aniyeah and Ashleigh planned to go on a quest to Mythical Island and find new creatures. We all went to pack and get our stuff. All of us packed and got snacks and drinks and went inside the transportation wardrobe (which seemed like hours). Me, Kayla, Leia, Aniyeah and Ashleigh arrived at Mythical Island and saw our unicorn friends called Emma, Natalia and Mouna. We fed them and gave them lots of kisses, but then we all saw a dragon! Aniyeah shrieked and the unicorns ran so we also ran all together.

Anoushka Rukengwa Ailpio (8)
Allen Edwards Primary School, Stockwell

The Missing Money Mystery

As I stepped into the town centre, a zooming van passed me. I span and hit my head on the poll. Just as my eyes adjusted, I saw a poster reading: 'Missing money, reward £100,000'. I rushed back to my house and told my friends, Liv, Katlyn, Maddie. They said they'd join me. We went to the bank to find some clues. There was a trail of money. The trail led to a white van, the one that zoomed past me. Liv had a theory, one that shocked me, Maddie and Katlyn.

"It could've been the people in the van."

Idil Mohamed Osman (10)
Allen Edwards Primary School, Stockwell

The Haunted Mansion

It was Halloween night. I had previously arranged for my friends, Zoe, Aaliyah and Yasmine, and I to meet up at the haunted mansion that I booked. We planned to play scary games such as Ouija board and many more. But one thing we did not know was the building was haunted with the spirits of the previous owners. As we set off to the destination, Zoe was trembling with fear of what could happen. Unexpectedly, whilst I was walking, I felt a cold, chilling sensation up my spine. We all decided to go back home since we were cowards.

Ruweda Nor (11)
Allen Edwards Primary School, Stockwell

Unicorn Seek

One snowy December day, I was playing with my friends Mary, Deborah, Isabella and Hannah. We were playing hide-and-seek in the garden. When I was trying to find a place to hide, something caught my eye. It was something bright, colourful and big. As I got closer, it started getting brighter and brighter. When I was so close, the shine started to burn my eyes. Then I found out what it was, it was a unicorn.

One hour later, the others found out. Later on, we were thinking of a name. I said Rose, we agreed and said yes!

Leah Chukwunyere-Jones (7)
Allen Edwards Primary School, Stockwell

Lucy Jay's Adventures!

I thought of such an evil machine that I would be top of the Evil List. I started working on it, straight away! 'The Earth Core', TEC for short. While I was busy making my project, this annoying brat for a superhero disturbed me. He was wearing a blindfold, which I thought was smart to do. Then he started to take bits of my machine. I was livid! I had to take action. He missed all of my painful shots, surprisingly. He then took out a device and stung me with it. I wasn't evil anymore, instead, I was good.

Elizabeth Ihaza (10)
Allen Edwards Primary School, Stockwell

The Diamond Heist

The wind blew in my face as I ran and hurdled over the gaps of the buildings. The backpack was extremely heavy, filled with diamonds. The helicopter chased me on the way to the hideout. I slid down a ladder and luckily, I lost the police when I sprinted into a dark alley next to a bar. The hideout was just above it. I sneaked in and displayed the riches to my accomplices. I heard the security alarm blaring, it was the police. I alerted my tired assistants and we escaped through the window. We were never seen again.

Claudia Yip (9)
Allen Edwards Primary School, Stockwell

My Wonderful Journey To The Moon

I woke up early in the morning and went to get ready for our trip to the moon. When I was ready, I went downstairs to have breakfast. After that, I went to the garage where our spaceship was and waited for my family. After a few minutes, I heard them talking so I put on the spaceship and quickly jumped up.

"In a few hours, we will be in space!" exclaimed my mum.

We all entered the spaceship and set off for space. When we arrived, we all kept our eyes on the moon. I enjoyed going to space.

Bisola Akinmejiwa (10)
Allen Edwards Primary School, Stockwell

Unicorn Land

I went through the imaginary portal that nearly made me blind to how bright it was. Once I went through, I was in shock, it was so beautiful and mythical. If my mum came, she would faint with so many cute, little unicorns which she calls creatures. I saw unicorns on very lush beds like a queen would sleep on. I felt like I was a unicorn. I thought they were extinct but they weren't. I could stay there all day without falling asleep as usual. And that was when I found out that my portal had gone away...

Oluwafunmilayo Ilori (9)

Allen Edwards Primary School, Stockwell

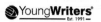

Lilly And Jayden And The Lost World

One day, two best friends, Lilly and Jayden, heard an urban legend that there was a portal in the forest, not too far away from them. So they decided to look for the portal.

One hour later, Jayden was bored so he ran and tripped over a rake. After that, a gleaming glow appeared and they gasped in fear. They cautiously stepped into it and appeared in a land full of monsters, aliens and then the portal closed.

A man called John came and said, "If you want to return, find the gemstones!"

Kevin Barrigah Benissan (9)
Allen Edwards Primary School, Stockwell

Candyland

Today was going to be the best day ever because we were going to Candyland. We were going to see real unicorns and ride real ponies! It would be so much fun! This morning, at 5am, I jumped out of bed and went to wake my parents up because I knew they would be excited too. We hurriedly got dressed and got into the car to drive to Candyland. We got there and it was so magical. There were candyfloss trees and lollipops. We found the unicorn trail and we stroked the unicorns. We wished it would never end.

Teoni Ranku (8)
Allen Edwards Primary School, Stockwell

Magic Board Game

I was playing with my friends, Alexis, the game was chess. My friend and I loved that game, we would play it from morning to night, but the only thing to stop us was chocolate. I loved chocolate as much as I loved chess. We were getting some when I saw the board game turn into a big, purple thing that you could go through. My friend and I went through and saw a whole new world ahead of us. We couldn't believe our eyes! It was an amazing world, but we kept it a secret between us!

Rehoboth Hailemariam (10)
Allen Edwards Primary School, Stockwell

The 77th Annual Demon Games

One day, I was running late for school when I tripped over a rock then tumbled down the hill and fell into a portal. I was whisked away at hyperspeed. I flew out, realising I was in The Hunger Games. But with demons.

"Wait, what demons?"

Yeah, demons, but that's not the worst thing. No weapons, just powers.

"What?"

"Three..."

"Wait!"

"Two..."

"Noooo!"

"One..."

"Please no!"

"Go!"

The Demogorgon killed all demons like a snap. A portal opened, I landed in my class. So did the Demogorgon, it was P7b versus the Prince of Demons. This was the final showdown!

Connor Maguire (11)

Bushes Primary School, Glenburn

The Meteor

I entered the gargantuan rocket, it was towering above me. I walked into the steel door and took a seat. There were three white metal seats, one for me, one for my pilot and one for my engineer. They walked in and took a seat.

John, my pilot, shouted, "Ready for take-off?"

"The meteor is ready, isn't it?"

"Taking off in three, two, one..."

The rocket took off and we were flying towards a meteor with a bomb in our ship to destroy the meteor.

"Captain, we are approaching the meteor," said John.

"Detonate the bomb now!" I shouted...

Enzo Thouard (11)
Bushes Primary School, Glenburn

The Graveyard

One day I woke up panting for breath. Then I realised I was in a graveyard. I looked up and saw the tombstone on my bed: 'RIP Sapphire died today'.

How did this happen? I'm alive right? I thought to myself. I started to sprint and came across a ghost.

"Hi, I'm Ghost Goo," it said.

"I'm Sapphire. I have to get home," I replied.

"Run to your bed and try to sleep!"

I did what Goo said. Although I ran as fast as I could, everything was gone. Ghost Goo, my bed/grave. "What do I do now?" I wondered.

Emily Barnes (11)

Bushes Primary School, Glenburn

The Shape-Shifter

Quickly, I darted into a building. I could hear footsteps and yelling behind me. I started to sprint. Until I heard a gunshot, then the world faded into darkness... Four hours later, I woke up in a tiny room. A bright light pierced my eyes. *Where am I?* I thought. A large figure walked in, he walked over. Speedily, I tried to transform.

"If I were you, I wouldn't try that. Those chains make it impossible to transform," he sneered.

"Let me go!" I yelled.

"Anyway, I'll let you get ready for your execution," he laughed.

I cried...

Emily Ralston (11)
Bushes Primary School, Glenburn

The Night Of The Rising

Every night at midnight in the spooky graveyard, the scary ghosts and zombies awoke from their coffins. One dark and gloomy night, they ventured off to a creepy, haunted house! This house had windows blocked by plywood. There they found a little girl. The chase was on... They followed the helpless girl through every room in the house. That continued until she secretly climbed out of a window, then she ran straight back to her house as fast as her little legs would carry her small body and never returned to that spooky house again, even when she was older.

Aeryn Morris Devlin (11)
Bushes Primary School, Glenburn

The Time Travel

It's finished! Oh hi, I didn't see you there! I just finished the time machine.

"Frebe! Come here!"

Frebe's a monkey. He's really smart. We have to get the time machine to the invention convention, which starts in... five minutes! We're going to be late. Quick, get in the time machine. Okay, and go! Oh no! I-It's malfunctioning. It's stopped! Let's get out, I don't think this is our dimension. Wow! Is that a unicorn? Is that a dragon on a lead like a dog? That means only one thing, mythical creatures are real in this dimension!

Owen Oates (11)
Bushes Primary School, Glenburn

Dream Or Not?

Smash! Monika woke up terrified. She got out her bed and tried to walk but she just collapsed onto the floor. Then she heard someone say, "Monika come here, it's Mum."
Monika was confused because it sounded nothing like her mum. She ran out of her room, stumbling over her feet. When she got to her mum's room she then realised that her mum was at her gran's. But then she felt a sharp pain in her leg. She collapsed. Something wrapped around her leg and she was pulled back into the room. *Slam!*

Cameron McIlwraith (11)
Bushes Primary School, Glenburn

The Shadow

Before I went to bed, I switched off the lights but I saw a weird shadow. Quickly, I switched it back on again but I was intrigued to put it off again. Every time I switched it off, the shadow appeared. Eventually, I ended up switching it on and off but the shadow came closer. I switched it on again but the shadow was still there. Slowly, I walked towards it, regretting every step and the next thing I remembered was darkness.

I woke up in a hospital. I switched off my light again and there was the shadow...

Lola Shanks (11)

Bushes Primary School, Glenburn

The Dark Figure

One dark night, a girl called Sarah was playing basketball with her friends, Talor, John, Jack. Quickly, John shot, it hit the rim and it fell into a pit of darkness. The ball got thrown back at them, they thought it was friend pranking them so they all went down until they sunk into their stomachs. A dark figure pranced towards them, they stumbled their way out. They didn't make it, she woke up in an abandoned house. The dark figure stumbled over to the wall and wrote, 'I know you're awake'.

Owen Waddell (11)
Bushes Primary School, Glenburn

The Mythical Creature

Ma used to tell me a story about a mythical creature and I never believed her until... One day when I was out in the forest, things were normal but I felt as though someone was watching me, a creature, an animal. Suddenly, I heard a bush rustling. After long thought, I decided to go and check it out. As I got closer and closer, I could see a brownish-coloured den. I felt as though I had to go in. I slowly walked closer, then went in. Ma was right, there was a mythical creature after all!

Emma Gelston (10)
Bushes Primary School, Glenburn

The Scyther

It was a dark and stormy night when Matt entered the house. He heard a noise on the top floor so he went to investigate. By the time he got up, there was a doll sitting in the corner. He went to pick it up when the doll grew scythes from its back and turned into a ghost! He lunged at Matt, so Matt swung his sword. It got stuck in the ghost so he pulled it out, causing it to explode, sending purple goo flying. Matt used his goo collector to collect some and he then left the house.

Nathan Rooney (11)
Bushes Primary School, Glenburn

Alien Attack

I have been on the space station for three weeks, and haven't seen anything strange until now. There's a weird object getting closer and closer to the space station. I'm starting to panic now, I have no signal so I can't ask anyone on Earth for help and I'm now certain it's not space junk. I decide that I should go out and see what it really is so I put my spacesuit on and go out. As I walk out, it turns to me, a green beam shines on me and pulls me in. It is aliens...

Dylan Brown (11)
Bushes Primary School, Glenburn

Halloween Night

On a stormy Halloween night, there was a little girl called Mia. She was very tired so she lay down on her bed. She woke up to a loud *bang* in the kitchen. Mia went down to check but nothing was there so she went back into her room and all of her toys had moved. Mia went back to sleep. All of a sudden, she woke back up at 9:30am and all her toys were down in the kitchen and there was spilt milk over them so her mum had to go and buy more of the same toys.

Leah Patterson (11)
Bushes Primary School, Glenburn

ET's Journey

One day in Boston, USA, ET was strolling about. He walked down a creepy alleyway, but he was used to that. He could see something was not right so he went to the problem. He saw a vicious dog, it ran like a gunshot. So he ran to try to stop the dog. ET ran, suddenly, he was floating. He went up and up and up. Suddenly, ET was in space, the place he came from. ET was happy but sad because he liked Boston. He liked helping people, now he couldn't.

Eilidh McCarter (11)
Bushes Primary School, Glenburn

The Rising

The further and darker we go into the Pacific Ocean, the louder the noise gets, but we keep seeing lots of fish until all of a sudden, there was a cave with glowing yellow eyes. We try to rise to the surface but we are boosted up by whatever it is. We go as fast as a cheetah to New York. We measure the monster, it is about 100 metres, not as big as the first one, that was 250m. This may be a huge fight. This is when we found out monsters were real.

Steven Grose (11)
Bushes Primary School, Glenburn

Power Ranger

Once upon a time in the year 3000, there lived a boy named Max. He was a Power Ranger superhero and Max was the Black Ranger. His friends were also Power Rangers. Thomas, the Red Ranger, Enzo the Green Ranger, Cammy the Blue Ranger and Connor, the White Ranger. Their arch-enemy was the evilest of them all! Together the friends had to work together to save the future.

Thomas Service (11)
Bushes Primary School, Glenburn

My Lucifer Is Lonely

Chloe stepped into the movers' van. Suddenly, she was driving to her new home... They arrived straight away Chloe darted up the stairs and hung her mirror. She loved her mirror.

A little while later, she was bored so she decided to play a game. "Take me to my hauntings where all my happiness ends..."

"Arghhhhh!"

Suddenly, a creepy, button-eyed, possessed girl appeared and muttered, "If you insist..."

When Chloe looked again, she was inside a dark haunted house. When she opened her mouth to scream, she felt claws around her ankles. Her life flashed before her very eyes.

Ella-Mae Jones (11)
Cheadle Primary School, Cheadle

The Flying Future

'Perilous prisoner escaped last night, thought to have vanished into thin air'. Olivia gasped at the thought that there were other worlds and not just her own! Unfortunately, as everyone knew, when you realised the truth, it would appear right in front of you. It shone like the moon on a dark night as Olivia disappeared through the mist. Cautiously, she stepped out into the unknown which looked strangely like her own world but with chocolate lakes and flying cars. As Olivia set out to find the prisoner, a passerby recommended she be careful, but she did not listen...

Emily Laws (11)
Cheadle Primary School, Cheadle

The Time-Travelling Human!

What was that? I turned round only to find what looked like some sort of portal. I'll tell you what I did. I jumped into it. I mean, what else was I supposed to do? Everything went hazy but finally, everything came into view. This world seemed strangely familiar, like I'd seen it before. Everyone walking round with gas masks. *What is going on?* I thought as I was dragged into hiding. The penny dropped. It was World War II. Suddenly, a bomb dropped and a gas mask was slapped on my face. This was what war felt like. Wow!

Esmee Clarke (10)
Cheadle Primary School, Cheadle

The Mystery

One day, some children from 5L went on a trip to a forest. Suddenly, five of the students went missing, so everyone split off to hunt for them. They said to meet in the middle of the forest at 1pm.

Another four more went missing, then six, then nine until there was only one girl left. She heard voices, suddenly children started screaming and then she saw shadows.

Five minutes later she found all the children, they said, "Pranked you!" They were playing a prank on her. They laughed when they told her, but then there was a big *bang*...

Emily Lefley (9)

Crab Lane Community Primary School, Higher Blackley

Sugar Sweet Land

Once, a girl called Sophie, who was a fighter, appeared in a land called Sugar Sweet Land. It was as big as Russia. First, she saw a big marshmallow tree, she stepped closer to it and then she went to the strawberry milkshake river. It was Rapunzel's hair. Then she felt like something was behind her, it was something giant and hairy. It was candyfloss. It started to attack Sophie but Sophie pushed the monster in the lake and Sophie won. Then some little fairies flew up to her and they gave her some sparkle dresses for a reward.

Zlata Strelkova (9)
Crab Lane Community Primary School, Higher Blackley

The Fairy Garden

It all started one strange morning when Princess Leah woke with a startle. As she looked around, she found she wasn't at home. She was in a dark cave. *Beep!* There was a noise. She looked around and saw a small fairy. Leah could not believe her eyes. She climbed up as a baby fairy asked her to follow them. Leah did not have a choice, she grabbed a young fairy's hand and followed along through the bushes and out into a small village. It was a fairy garden, Leah had a hard decision and she decided to stay.

Darcie-May Deadman (9)

Crab Lane Community Primary School, Higher Blackley

Martian Encounter

On the darkest night of December, I went into a space jet and landed on the planet Mars. As I was walking, I saw a creepy shadow. When I got closer, I saw a weird object. I was scared as I got closer, I decided to go back to my space jet but something was following me. It was super fast so it got to my space jet.

"Don't worry, I'm not harmful," said the alien, wanting to play a game.

But first he told me his name was Gerry. It was really fun.

"Thank you Gerry, I had fun!"

Fikunayomi Junaid (7)

Crab Lane Community Primary School, Higher Blackley

Detective Mayhem

One day, my friend called me on my phone to tell me that villains were attacking the palace. I quickly put on my detective outfit. When I got to the palace, nobody was there. Were they inside? The guards were fast asleep. There were stink bombs everywhere. I tried not to step on them. The queen told me all about the mischievous villains. I caught them but they ran away. I had to make a plan. I finally caught them. After the celebration, we had a feast with the queen. Once again, with my detective skills, I did it!

Jomiloju Junaid (8)
Crab Lane Community Primary School, Higher Blackley

Buddy Saves Pablo The Dog

On a planet far away, Buddy the Superhero lived in his man cave. He flew away the next day to Earth and crashed into a wall. *Boom!* That was what everybody heard. A homeless dog called Pablo was there. Buddy brought Pablo to his man cave so then Buddy got Pablo healthy again. Pablo was the lucky dog. I guess he was not skinny anymore. He was just right. Everybody loved him but Buddy was the favourite because he saved the little dog.

Kyron Downie (8)

Crab Lane Community Primary School, Higher Blackley

Fire

In the ink-black heart of the unsightly northern forest stands a house that once belonged to a wealthy, though loathsome family. The house itself was a magnificent manor, until... Wednesday 31st October 1784, Halloween, the darkest day for that family, the day they disappeared. The day they left, the house began crumbling, the columns giving way, the walls splintering in despair; it became a hideous sight, surrounded by a tranquil silence, with a sinister air to it. Inside, the walls had holes in them, one wall in particular, the hole inside was an eerie swirling mass of purple fire...

Leah

Ennerdale CE Primary School, Ennerdale Bridge

Mission 54

"We need to get out of here!" I demanded. "We've been here for 27 days so we better get going."
Bang! A cal 32 bullet whizzed past my head.
"We're definitely not here alone," I said to myself. I picked up my AK-47 and threw it on the shotgun and got in the jeep. I put my foot on the throttle. I opened the door, I saw the figure with the gun, he was around 7ft and he was wearing black. *Bang!* I shot a dozen bullets at him, he lay dead on the ground. *Eat that*, I thought.

Edward
Ennerdale CE Primary School, Ennerdale Bridge

Shoot

All I was doing was sitting on a park bench when I fell into a dark abyss. I was extremely confused. I wasn't surprised, after all, it was Manhattan we're talking about.

All I said was... "Shoot."

When I landed, it was some sort of cube I was in. I still had my sandwich so I didn't care. I kind of wandered around. It wasn't exactly exciting. *It's just a cube?* is what I thought but as I walked around I noticed writing on the walls. It was minuscule but noticeable. It said to kick the wall. I did...

Sam Wagstaff (10)

Ennerdale CE Primary School, Ennerdale Bridge

Kidnapped

"Help!" I cry with terror.

All that I can remember is a tall, lanky man covered in black who hit me with something, I can't really remember what. Somehow I think I'm in a van. I am thinking to myself, *what if there are other people in here with me?* I am awfully terrified, too terrified to look, I think I'm going to brave it. As I look around, there are bodies all around me; hung from thin, tied ropes, banging off the sides of the van with merlot-coloured blood on the floor... Do you think I will survive?

Jaydn-Ema Durham
Ennerdale CE Primary School, Ennerdale Bridge

Big Foot

Crash! Bang! We were shipwrecked in the Mediterranean Sea near a small island around fifty metres away from the jagged rocks poking out of the rough, unforgiving sea. My only hope was to get to the island, but how? I sprang into action and I caught a turtle, tied it to a barrel on board the ship and then started swimming to the shore. As I reached the shore it was beginning to get dark so I knew I had to find shelter for the night. Suddenly there was a loud roar coming from the towering trees. Would I survive?

Marcus Dean (10)
Ennerdale CE Primary School, Ennerdale Bridge

New Year's Eve Surprise

It was the night before New Year's Eve and we had decided to camp on Ben Nevis in Scotland for the new year. I was up here with my dad and the views so far were beautiful, however, it was already dark. I was so tired from a day of climbing so we set up our camp and halfway through setting up my tent, a violent gale blew the tents away and also started an avalanche. We had packed some sledges for the snowy area of the mountain, we put them down, sat down and raced for our lives.

Saul Rowan Richardson Shail (10)

Ennerdale CE Primary School, Ennerdale Bridge

A Wonderful Dream!

Daydreaming, Lily meandered towards a pink, wooden door. Before her were small, twinkling figures floating on the breeze.

"Fairies!" she gasped.

Startled, she ran, they followed, whispering and giggling. Water tumbled over the cliffs in front of her, and pooled around the feet of a surprising herd of unicorns. Her eyes widened in disbelief and her mouth hung open. Just then, she noticed movement in the water. Long, wavy hair travelled down the female's back until it met her fishy tail. Magic overwhelmed her until...

"Lilly!" she heard the distant call of her mother.

"Coming!" called the beautiful, sleepy girl.

Ava Carter

Granby Primary School, Aylestone

The Enchanted Paper

Jake was a boy who loved writing. Unfortunately, he'd run out of paper, so decided to try the new shop in town, 'The Enchanted Paper'.

"What do you want?" screeched the grotesque-looking woman behind the counter.

"J-Just some paper," stammered Jake.

"Take this..." she muttered and threw a pad at him.

"Th-Thank you," whimpered Jake.

At home, Jake began to write a story with his new paper when he left to get a drink. To his utter amazement, when he re-entered his own words had been replaced 'Karro Udomo'... he whispered, at which point, thick green smoke enveloped him...

Ethan Patel (8)
Granby Primary School, Aylestone

The Orange Visitor

One spooky night in the Howard household, James was about to go to bed but suddenly, *bang!* James heard one of the doors slam. He was terrified. He knew he was home alone. *Stomp!* It was close. *Stomp!* It was outside his door. *Whoosh!* His door swung open.

"Arghhhhh!"

It was orange, tall, scary and loud. It started walking towards him. The orange light started getting brighter. *Stomp!* James' phone disappeared. His laptop fell to the floor.

"We've all the electronics we need, we'll leave now, bye," said a creepy voice next to him.

The orange light disappeared. *Whoosh!*

Jack Bender (10)
Granby Primary School, Aylestone

The Revenge Of Cross Claw

I'm watching TV and apparently, a monster called Cross Claw has escaped.

"Keep your doors locked!" warns the news reporter.

Ignoring his warning, I walk outside and looking around to see if it's out here. Nothing. Walking back inside, I make one last check, nope. So, I'm going to bed. It's midnight, and something is scratching on my door. *It's probably the cat*, I think. The scratching stops and growling begins. Shakily, I walk over to my door, looking through the peephole. I see Cross Claw! The door breaks open and it storms in. It grabs me...

Tayla Goldsmith-Noyes (10)
Granby Primary School, Aylestone

The Mystery Of The Missing Motorbike

Detective Johnny English and Assistant Teddy walked through the immense crowd of people watching the fascinating Hamley's toy parade on Regent Street. They walked in the opposite direction of the parade. They discussed the peculiar mystery of the missing motorbike. One night, all of a sudden in the space of half an hour, the motorbike disappeared. Nobody was in the area at the time. It was a dead night. Detective Johnny English and Assistant Teddy were tremendously bewildered. They had no idea what they faced. This was only the start of this provoking story. Would they solve the mystery?

Umayr Mahomed (10)
Granby Primary School, Aylestone

The Tree House

Brook and her parents moved to a new village called Aylestone. At the bottom of their garden was an eerily derelict tree house. The sullen twilight smothered the sky. Brook should've been in bed, instead, she ventured into darkness. As she crept down the garden, the tree house's shadow hunched over her like a ghoul. Brook climbed the creaky, broken ladder. Once inside, she heard a peculiar noise, a piano. She tiptoed further into the room. The moon's light illuminated the piano in the corner. To her surprise, there sat a silvery, cloaked figure. It never bothered to look up.

Jasmine Jade Rossington (10)
Granby Primary School, Aylestone

Super Baby!

My baby brother is no ordinary baby... he is Super Baby! By day, he drinks milk and poos in his nappy, by night he battles the evil Captain Cucumber. On a dreary night, Captain Cucumber embarked on his greatest plan, to rob City Bank.

"Come on you stupid gherkins... hurry!" ordered Captain Cucumber.

The gherkins placed the last bag of money on the truck. A silhouette appeared.

"It's Super Baby!" shrieked the gherkins.

"Goo, goo, ga, ga!"

In a flash, the gherkins were rounded up, Captain Cucumber was arrested and Super Baby was home just in time for a bottle.

Ruby Quinnell (9)
Granby Primary School, Aylestone

Snowy The Dragon

Once there was a dragon called Snowy. Unlike your usual fire-breathing dragon, Snowy couldn't light fires or toast marshmallows. All he could do was stop things drastically melting. One night, on a cold winter's eve, Snowy saw the most beautiful shooting star he had ever seen. To be fair, he hadn't seen many before. He wished he could be a normal, useful dragon who didn't freeze everything. The next day, Snowy didn't feel any different. He still had cold blood, he even tested. However, when he walked outside. Everyone crowded around him with joy. His wish had unbelievably come true.

Scarlet Dalton (10)
Granby Primary School, Aylestone

The No-Answer Forest

A shelf-sized and nameless robot walked through the forest. His red and blue reflective materials shining at things like cat's eyes. This small, misunderstood robot had no understanding of what his name was or why he was here. Suddenly, an immense cylinder rose from the ground, uprooting a whole circle of trees even though it wasn't out of the ground. The robot spotted a large opening in the cylinder and carelessly advanced into it. Soon, he was rocketing through the tunnel of a million lights and landing in a secret bunker to find out his name was Zultrex. Zultrex fainted.

Edward Palmer (9)
Granby Primary School, Aylestone

Mr Tigglewiggle Hits The Fairground

Mr Tigglewiggle was ready for an adventure. He was visiting a mysterious fairground above his trampoline, where you could jump from ride to ride. It was big and dazzling. The music was loud, exciting and rhythmic. On the gigantic, big wheel, he gasped as suddenly he was being chased by an identical twin! On the waltzers, he spun round to get away. Leaping onto the spooky ghost train, the cheeky twin was there again! He decided to face his fears and confront the twin. Suddenly, he realised there were mirrors around the fairground and realised that the twin was him.

Louis Nthakomwa-Cassidy (8)

Granby Primary School, Aylestone

The Legend Of The Karate Portal

Once there was a boy who dreamt of trying karate. "Hi-yah!" cried the boy.

His name was Bic.

He sped to his dad, saying, "Please can I try karate?"

His dad said, "Okay."

Bic screamed, "Yes!"

Once he opened the door, he saw lots of people wearing different coloured belts. The sensei bowed, Bic bowed also. Once they started, Bic lost interest in doing the same thing ten times. Something caught his eye, it was a door with weird characters. He crept to the door, opened it and looked inside. A random purple thing sucked him in it...

Toyel Tojo (10)
Granby Primary School, Aylestone

Crazy Cats

Our new house had a catflap. One day, two black cats appeared. We kept them, but they were very strange. They would disappear, so one day, I decided to follow them. One peered through a neighbour's front window, miaowed at the other, then the other climbed a drainpipe and jumped through a bedroom window. Next the cat inside the house ran into the downstair's front room and scooped a goldfish back into its bowl! On our way back, the cats helped an elderly lady with a white stick cross the road. Guide cats? Cats that help fish? Whatever next?

Theo James Brown (11)
Granby Primary School, Aylestone

My New Pet

It was getting darker as I walked home from my friend's house and I think I may have taken the wrong turning. I could see an old house. I knocked on the door to get directions. The door opened but nobody was there. A dog appeared from nowhere.
"Can I help?" the dog said.
"What? You talk!" I said.
"Yes," replied the dog.
This was crazy!
"I'm lost."
"I will show you the way home on one condition, that you will be my owner."
"Of course," I replied.
"Then follow me."
He took me home. I love my dog.

Aimee Richards (10)
Granby Primary School, Aylestone

Alice The Unicorn Believer

Alice had a secret, so one night she sat with her mum and said, "I believe in unicorns."
Mum smiled and replied, "If you climb a rainbow, you will find a unicorn."
Alice was determined to find one. So the next day, a rainbow came. Alice started her adventure so she hiked to the end of the rainbow. Then she started to climb up the colourful arch. Upon reaching the top, she saw the most magnificent thing in the world, it was a unicorn. She couldn't believe her eyes, so she rode it home and kept it forever and ever.

Neve Pritchard-Doughty (9)
Granby Primary School, Aylestone

Planet Of The Cats

One night, two sleepy cats called Spaghetti and Clinton dreamt they were flying to the moon, but they drifted off course to a massive cat planet which was shaped like a cat head with a tail. They landed on the planet and saw lots of alien cats, they all had one ear and two tails. Spaghetti, Clinton and the other cats played with the catnip tail and the electric string which drove them crazy. Suddenly, Spaghetti and Clinton heard their owner calling from Earth so they waved goodbye to the cats and flew back. Then they both woke for breakfast.

Ellie Zulerons (10)
Granby Primary School, Aylestone

Sherlock The Hero

It all started when Bob the farmer, AKA Snowbird Bandit, wanted to rob a jewellery store. But he did not know that he was going to the store where Sherlock lived. Sherlock was really clever, hence he decided to trap the bandit with his awesome plan. As soon as the bandit stepped a foot into the store, he skidded across the floor and crashed into a wall, because Sherlock had poured some oil at the door. When Sherlock heard the noise, he rushed downstairs and handcuffed him and called the cops who took him into prison. Bob learned his lesson.

Joash Sam Samuel (10)
Granby Primary School, Aylestone

Different World

All of a sudden, I woke up, it was loud, bright, everywhere had colour. I didn't recognise this place. There was something different. I recognised it as soon as I stepped outside. I was in a parallel universe. I saw dogs with cat bodies, people who looked like monkeys, houses that looked like trees, holes in the road and the sky was purple. Worst of all, cars looked like planes. This wasn't home, Earth was, Planet Earth was, I needed to go home. Then out of nowhere, this world suddenly ended. I was home. I was glad it was over.

Jaydan James Whitmore (10)
Granby Primary School, Aylestone

A Freaky Sight!

At first, it was all a blur. Jamie stepped out of the time machine, his head still fuzzy from the journey. The setting in front of him seemed pretty familiar. Then, it hit him! It was Earth. His hometown in fact. But wait... where were the humans? All Jamie could see were buildings. They weren't busy as usual. It was silent, like a ghost town. He walked into the building closest to him, it was full of aliens. Green ones, ones with millions of eyes, and so on. Then they saw Jamie. They darted at him and there was darkness...

Grace Amelia Bryning (10)
Granby Primary School, Aylestone

The Sad Ball

The ball was sad as he never got chosen to be used in any of the Premier League matches, he didn't even get picked for training. His dream was to get saved by Kasper Schmeichel in a game, Leicester versus Liverpool, but his dream didn't look like it was going to happen. One Saturday morning, the referee came to pick the ball for the match and he finally picked Sad Ball. He couldn't believe his luck! The game kicked off, he was getting kicked all over the pitch. His dream came true, he got saved by Schmeichel and Leicester won!

Josh Marvell (10)
Granby Primary School, Aylestone

Where? Why? How?

James Miller casually strolled along the surface of the deserted land of Feltas B6. It had been like that for centuries. It often had earthquakes but this one was major. James continued his thoughts about why he was here, where he was and how he didn't know the name of this planet. At this moment, the ground tore open and a shiny, silver pod flew out, rocketing across the sky and circling James in an eerie way. The pod turned into a steep dive but about 150 feet from the ground, the pod released gas which knocked James out.

Maxwell Cheung-Ross (10)
Granby Primary School, Aylestone

Life Of An Odd Child

I crept up through the corridor, shading my skin from the other children's eyes, and waited for the laughing to start but something else caught their eye. They were giggling and pointing at something or someone else. It was a child, a child like me. With the same condition as me and she was trying not to cry like when they started chuckling at me and I started weeping. I did something quite daring then, but now I felt good for doing it. I showed all the skin on my arms and took my scarf off. Something never done before.

Karin Karzan Karim (11)

Granby Primary School, Aylestone

The Night At The Graveyard

The clock struck midnight and the graveyard was pitch-black. Nobody was anywhere near. A humming sound began and coffins started to rise slowly. The dead bodies walked out of their coffins. It all seemed like a dream and not a very nice one. All of a sudden, the floor was shaking but the dead bodies weren't. What was happening, what was going on? When, finally, it all stopped, there was a girl lying right in the middle of the graveyard. She had a name on her T-shirt and that was the name on the grave of the empty coffin...

Maisy Dalton (10)
Granby Primary School, Aylestone

The Mermaid Catastrophe

Once there was a girl called Ella and she lived near the beach. So one day, she went down to the beach by herself. She was quite happily walking along the sand when she saw an unusual tail flicker out of the water. She got closer. It was a dazzling mermaid stuck in a bush of seaweed. She gasped in horror. Ella swam as fast as she could and held her breath underwater whilst she untangled the mermaid. The mermaid thanked her so very much. Every time Ella came down to the beach, she would joyfully play with the mermaid.

Emily Dilkes (9)
Granby Primary School, Aylestone

The Secret Door

Last night, something peculiar happened. I woke up because I heard a noise so I went to investigate. It led me to a wooden door that I had never opened before. I ventured into the mysterious room. The door creaked as it opened. On a table, sat a bag full of money with my name on it. I grabbed it greedily. Inside was two hundred pounds! Suddenly, a man appeared out of nowhere. The man hit me with his fist, in my jaw. I blacked out.

I woke up and sat there bewildered. My mind was racing incredibly fast.

Ava Francess Brown (9)
Granby Primary School, Aylestone

Zaira And The Netted Dolphins

It all began when Zaira was at the beach. She was playing catch with her brother. He got tired and rested on the beach chairs. Zaira decided to go in the sea. She started to swim deeper and deeper until she saw a herd of dolphins. They were her favourite animals. Zaira began to swim closer until she was there and she was panicking. They were trapped. She saw some sharp pieces of wood and cut the net so then the dolphins could be free. She did that and now she was happy because they were free and safe.

Karishma Garratt (8)
Granby Primary School, Aylestone

Space Dragon

So the dragon and the spaceman were best friends until one day, they had an argument and it didn't end well. The dragon turned into the spaceman and the spaceman turned into the dragon.
They said, "We've switched bodies!"
"OMG, so I am the dragon."
"And I am the spaceman, oh no!"
The spaceman and the dragon were the most upset they'd ever been in their lives so they started having some fun and they both said, "This is the best day of my life."
They finally switched back.

Miller Sweet (10)
Granby Primary School, Aylestone

Mike The Hero

Mike read a book about Termon. Nobody had ever seen him. Mike knew that he could catch the creature because he had a speed jet. Termon lived in Bolt Sea. Many people would wait all day and night to see him but that never happened. So Mike went to the sea and jumped into the speed jet excitedly. His boat swam as fast as a cheetah could run. Mike was getting closer and closer to Termon until he was right behind him. Mike pressed the blue net button and caught Termon. But what was he going to do now?

Lena Maria Pigan (10)
Granby Primary School, Aylestone

Tom's Space Mission To The Moon

NASA spent £500billion on metal to make a rocket for Tom. His rocket set off on the count of three, two, one... There was a clatter but it was okay. He slept for a minute or two. He woke to find he was in an asteroid belt. *Bang! Boom! Shatter!* He was safe. He woke up again to find he went past the moon. He clicked all the buttons but couldn't find the exit button. He found he was in front of a black hole. This was it. He found the button and turned around to Earth. Phew! Yay!

Terrence Vooi (8)

Granby Primary School, Aylestone

The Mystery

One day, I walked down the trench because it was my day. On the way down to meet my captain, he told me to look everywhere for a specific body. I said okay, but I was a little bit startled at what he had said. I had so many questions like, *why did he need it?* Then I saw the body. Then I went over and it disappeared. Then I went back to find my captain. I found him dead on the floor. Just then, a Jerry popped out, then loads and then I was scared. One shot, two...

Jack Griffin (11)
Granby Primary School, Aylestone

The Unicat

I stepped out my front door, with amazement, I saw a cat with a horn. I didn't know what it was. Was it a unicat of some sort? I could not resist but took it in my house. It looked dirty so I washed it. After drying it, I saw its horn glow with the sun and it went all rainbow. Its eyes were glowing too and turned into star shapes. The next day, I took it to the vets and they told me that she was rare. When I went out, it caught everyone's attention. I loved her.

Yasmine Bhihe (10)
Granby Primary School, Aylestone

The World Of All Worlds

I ventured into the darkness, only to discover a world full of... well, everything! Dinosaurs, war and even modern-day animals. It was like all times had come together as one! It was amazing. I loved it. I looked around, I ran in but it was overrun with cavemen. It was a great surprise to keep on looking. In the distance, I saw a volcano. I ran towards it, dodging the shots of the war and I knew that there was a lot more to this place than it seemed.

Jack Newton (10)
Granby Primary School, Aylestone

Boodicca And The Pignappers

Boodicca was a pig. She went to the park once but a pignapper (who was actually a bear) kidnapped her from Hoffel Town and put her in a cell. Two days later, he told her he saved her because Evil Pig was trying to take her because he was gonna build a robot to kill everyone.

He said, "Do you want to team up?"

She said yes and they made the best superhero team ever. Now Boodicca is known as the saviour for destroying Evil Pig forever.

Poppy Sone (10)

Granby Primary School, Aylestone

The Lady Who Always Wore Black

In the middle of the forest, there was a haunted, dark, abandoned house. In that house lived an old lady that always wore black. One day, at night, we decided to go in that house in the forest. In that forest were lots of snakes, scorpions, black widows, poisonous ants and poisonous frogs. We approached the house and saw a lady in black, standing there by her front door, waiting for us suspiciously...

Paige Tebbutt (10)
Granby Primary School, Aylestone

Doughnuts And Dimensions

Vilinda stayed behind at the Doom stadium after her friends left to practise her powers.

Duckdoughnut appeared from nowhere with his army and surrounded Vilinda like a wall. He was sure after defeating her, he would rule the world. She was the last one to get.

"What are you doing here?" said Vilinda.

"Erm... here to destroy you!" said Duckdoughnut with his fire-shooting gadget.

He blasted towards Vilinda, little did he know she could control fire and using her hands, Vilinda pushed back onto Duckdoughnut and his villains with such force, it sent them to another dimension. *Whoosh!*

"Yes!"

Aslı Çetin (9)

Grange Park Primary School, Winchmore Hill

The Amazing Pebble

A girl named Ellie was playing about on the decks, clutching treasure. 'The treasure' was an amazing pebble her granny called Ocean gave Ellie when she was five. She was eight now. The pebble was bouncing about on Ellie's chest; she'd made it into a necklace. Suddenly, Ellie heard a great *thud* on the deck. *Whoosh! Splash!* The weight of the thing blew Ellie overboard.

In the water, Ellie felt for her necklace... it was gone. Panicking, she looked down and there it was *glistening*, just within her reach. She reached down. To her amazement, she saw a mermaid tail.

Christiana Maria Christofi (9)
Grange Park Primary School, Winchmore Hill

Danger Dave

Danger Dave is a detective. One day, he was walking through an abandoned alleyway when he spotted a man with a girl stuffed inside his backpack. *Bang!* The man dematerialised. Dave ran over and dropped through a hole. When Dave landed, he saw the man holding the girl. *Smash!* Dave hit him as hard as a hammer. He gulped, grabbed the girl and scurried through the hole. When the two people got to Cockfosters Parade, where she was taken, the girl spotted her mum. Her and her super saviour ran to her.
"Thank you," she exclaimed gratefully.
Danger Dave vanished.

Harry Stylianou (9)
Grange Park Primary School, Winchmore Hill

The Pollution Solution

"Litter is killing so many innocent creatures."
Daniel turned off the television, tears violently
rolling out of his eyes. He felt the front door slam
shut behind him. The rain whipped into his face.
Daniel hurried to the local beach and dived into
the green, dirty water. Daniel edged forward.
Something was screaming for help. The petrified
boy looked above him. Entangled in a plastic
bottle; a wailing fish. Daniel hastily removed it and
set it free. From then on, Daniel spread the word to
his community. Just like you can do! Together, we
can make a big great change.

Jacob Polak (10)
Grange Park Primary School, Winchmore Hill

Jungle Bonanza

Stumbling through the jungle, a warm and inviting aroma awoke his tired senses. Gareth followed the smell until he was stopped in his tracks. There before him stood an ancient stone village. Intrigued, Gareth moved closer and closer. *Bash!* Suddenly, he tumbled down a hill where he was met by the most hideous creature. He tried to run but he was trapped in the hole. He cried for help, then suddenly, a dark silence overshadowed the gaping hole. Gareth saw a strong, fierce man above him. The monster hurried away, leaving Gareth in the hole. Then he woke up.

Reggie Perkins
Grange Park Primary School, Winchmore Hill

The Unknown Adventure!

Lucy and Jessica decided to go on an adventure. So they went. Until they found a deep, dark cave. So they went in. *What fun that will be*, they thought. They got a torch and stepped in. A few moments later, they found a light so they blew out their torch and followed the light which led to a steep pit. *Should we go down?* they wondered. *Maybe*, they wondered again. So they decided to go down. Until Lucy slipped and went sliding down the pit. Finally, they were down and there they found a dead body.
"Why's that there?"

Daria Valizadeh (10)
Grange Park Primary School, Winchmore Hill

The Cat Burglar

Crash! I woke up with a start. I crept downstairs and was met by an alarming sight. The Christmas tree and all its decorations were strewn across the floor. Curtains had been ripped off their rings. Oh no! The house had been burgled! I frantically searched for any missing objects. Suddenly, a glint of green caught my eye from underneath the moving curtains. Was the burglar still here? I froze in fear. I wanted to scream but my throat went dry. Missile-like, a black and white deadly ball of fluff launched itself at me. Had I found my cat burglar?

Amelia Marrison-Claffey (9)
Grange Park Primary School, Winchmore Hill

The Great Rescue Dog!

Once, a dog named Paddywack lived in an abandoned farm. One day, he heard a cry for help. As soon as he heard the noise, he ran to it as fast as he could. He realised it was a kid and he was injured. Paddywack started barking. *Woof woof!* People came running to him. They saw the injured boy and called an ambulance. Staff came and took the boy away in the ambulance. Paddywack was asked if he would like to be the child's pet. "Woof!" replied Paddywack.

And Paddywack, the kid and his parents all lived happily and safely.

Nihar Vaidya (9)

Grange Park Primary School, Winchmore Hill

Alien Hero Of The World

Aliens and humans live together on Earth. There was an alien called Anastasi, he was ten years old. A couple of days after his tenth birthday, there was a ginormous black hole, it was terrifying. Anastasi knew if it pulled a certain amount of people in, it got bigger. So Anastasi jumped into the black hole to prevent it from swallowing everybody and everything. Anastasi was extremely brave with his giant hammer, he destroyed the black hole and everyone fell out onto the grass. Anastasi the alien became famous and he made the world a better place.

Anastasi Kyriacou (10)
Grange Park Primary School, Winchmore Hill

The Sleepover Mystery

One day a little girl, aged 12, was playing a game with her four friends. They were the most popular kids in school. The girl treated her friend as dolls, she was in control of everything.

One stormy night they had a sleepover. They all fell asleep, apart from the leader.

They woke up the next morning and couldn't find her. She was missing. They went out of the cabin to her house and couldn't open the door. They looked through the window and saw blood splattered all over the wall. They never found what happened to her...

Antonia Charalambous (10)
Grange Park Primary School, Winchmore Hill

What Happened?

I stepped out through a dark, mysterious portal, sending me into a huge tropical forest. Dinosaurs were walking around like nothing had happened. Strange people were floating up above the trees and hitting them, causing hard-shelled coconuts to drop on top of my warm, silky hair. There was a suspicious line that on one side it was raining, and on the other side, it was a hot, sunny desert. Suddenly, a loud scream echoed from the raining side to the sunny side. It had wings as long as a plane and a very short tail. It wasn't a pterodactyl!

Jing-Yang Koh (9)
Grange Park Primary School, Winchmore Hill

This Can Only Mean One Thing

Suddenly, he sees a dark old haunted house. He walks inside curiously. The house is all broken and dirty. There is dust all over the floor and skeletons on tables. Suddenly, he hears a noise as loud as an earthquake, it is roaring and squeaking. All doors close, lights turn on and off repeatedly. He feels scared, nervous and alone. Everything stops, lights turn off completely, there is silence, he stands as still as a statue. The ghost is an old friend of his. He says, "Join me," then disappears.

This only means ghosts exist!

Nadeem Ezzedine (9)

Grange Park Primary School, Winchmore Hill

The Desolate Island

I woke up to the sound of waves crashing into my body. I looked around to find my sister and I were stranded on a desolate island. As the realisation set in, I screamed, waking up my sister and every creature on the island. My sister jumped up in horror.

"Where are we?" yelled my sister, her voice echoing around the island.

A small orange lizard ran up to us. My sister stuck her tongue out, she angered it and I noticed a trail of fire.

"Run!" I screamed.

We jumped into a massive shell and got teleported back home.

Amelie Hon (9)

Grange Park Primary School, Winchmore Hill

The Big Chase

This story is about three friends who went into a store to steal jewellery. Unfortunately, the police were hunting down the three friends and chased after them. While they were trying to get away, the secret police detective had been on the lookout for the armed men whose mission was to terrorise the whole community. The armed men had caused a lot of disaster and pain to the people and the entire community at large. The detective discovered the hidden safe house of the armed men and arrested them and jailed them all.

Omotobi Olulode (9)

Grange Park Primary School, Winchmore Hill

Superbob

Superbob has a mission to save the children from being bored but first, he needs to find them. Thankfully, he has a sidekick, Littlebob. One day, Littlebob spots a sad dad who tells him his son is always bored and then Littlebob tells him he knows how to help his son. All he needs to do is to get in touch with Superbob. Superbob sends a very special password that will allow his son to play a new game that Superbob created, called it Fortnite.
The game was successful and no child was bored again.

Kemal Yilmaz (9)
Grange Park Primary School, Winchmore Hill

The Aliens' Secret Mission

An alien saw a purple portal that he was so tempted to step in and explore but something felt weird. He sensed something dangerous and bad in this magical portal. He was so curious to see what was in there. Just at that very second, he felt that strange feeling again, he had to jump in so he did. He used his head vision, he heard a sound and a strange rhyme. His heart started pounding, his feet trembling, his feet quaking, his body quaking and shaking. His teeth were quivering. What could it be?

Emmerson Camp (10)
Grange Park Primary School, Winchmore Hill

Lava Girl - Criminal Or Hero?

Fiercely, I bolted through the path so I could get home quickly, but on my way home, something suspicious caught my eye. It was the most wanted criminal in the whole world murdering someone. Suddenly, the criminal saw me and I ran away as fast as my legs could carry me. Luckily, Lava Girl, the superhero, came and chased the criminal. She was running as quick as a cheetah and finally caught the criminal and shot him with her laser-shooting eyes. He became unconscious and she took him to prison.

Talia Penn (9)

Grange Park Primary School, Winchmore Hill

Toy Alert

I was walking into my bedroom after a long day at school and my bedroom was messy and all my toys were everywhere. So that night, I stayed up all night to see who was doing this. When my mum tucked me in, I got my torch all ready to see who was doing this. I could not believe my eyes, it was my toys. My teddies were looking out the window, my dinosaurs were having a chat with Mr Piggy. So I want to say something to everyone reading this: your toys are alive, believe in them.

Jeyda Dervish (9)
Grange Park Primary School, Winchmore Hill

Violet's Adventure

When my parents died, I lived on my own. Then one weird day, I was kidnapped. I was taken to this really strange place. As I stepped in, my body froze. The house was dark and there was no colour. While I stepped into the room, something pierced behind me. When I turned around, an old-looking china doll was glaring at me. She was holding a knife that was made from plastic. I tried to run but the china doll was holding me Suddenly, I whacked the doll with my belt and I ran...

Havin Uludag (9)

Grange Park Primary School, Winchmore Hill

Desert Island

Luke, Liam and Leo went to an abandoned island. Liam was an expert so he was in charge but Leo did not like it so he left. Leo got lost and tried to make a fire hut but he was useless without Liam. Then a monkey came. The monkey was leading Leo back to the hut. On the way Leo found gold in an old tree. He took it back to the hut. Luke and Liam were making a boat to leave the island to go home and let the monkey come and that was the best day.

Ollie Tini (10)
Grange Park Primary School, Winchmore Hill

The Most Powerful Headmaster In The World

One day, a brother and sister called Alex and Sophie went to America for one month. After lots of travelling, they came back to school. Their friends sounded weird so they tried to find out what had happened. There was a new headmaster who had taken over their school. So they met him, he looked strange and scary.

He said, "Look into my eyes."

A boy called Ethan said, "Did you like the new headmaster?"

They said yes but looked confused. They found out that he was hypnotising everyone. So they told their friends and then chased him away.

Haleemah Ali (9)

Greenhill Academy, Glodwick

The Investigation's End

One gloomy night, a robber passed by a jewellery shop but didn't know a spy was watching. She recorded everything. The robber stole every single diamond. The spy hid in the bushes. The robber left the shop but didn't have the jewellery. The spy felt confused. She definitely didn't see him drop the sack. Suddenly, she looked around and nobody was there. So she jumped out in fear but noticed the robber had left without his mask. The spy followed a trail of jewellery that led her to a note but it was blank. She couldn't investigate.

Inaya Chowdury (7)
Greenhill Academy, Glodwick

The Princess Who Gets Saved

Once upon a time, there was a princess called Jenfer who lived in a castle with soldiers protecting her from kidnappers because Jenfer could not protect her own body. Then a few hours later, Jenfer walked with her best friend. Jenfer was a little nervous because she was on her own with no one. Kidnappers came and stole Jenfer's handbag. After that, a superhero came and got the handbag and then the superhero stated to Jenfer, "Come, I'll give you a lift to your castle."
Jenfer said, "Thank you very much."

Somaya Iqbal (7)
Greenhill Academy, Glodwick

Space Maze

A bright light shines before him. Bravely stepping into the mysterious portal, he finds stunning stars surrounding him. There are no other explanations, he knows it is space. Suddenly surrounded by a group of people lined across, a beep sounds. Pushing and shoving people run past him. He wants answers as to what is going on so he tries to catch up to them. A winding path forms to what seems an endless maze where a race is taking place. Nearly towards the end of the finish line, he feels someone from behind coming for him. Then he wakes up.

Shuaib Hussain (9)

Greenhill Academy, Glodwick

The Magical Journey

One lovely, sunny day, a family of unicorns lived in a sparkly castle and their names were Spark, the mother; Lily, the newborn; and Rose, the little sister who was two years old. Next, they went for a walk in the city. After that, they went into the Amazon rainforest. Something magical happened... The Amazon rainforest went all sparkly and the waterfall went all rainbow. Their unicorn horns went all magical. When Spark touched it on something, it turned into herself. They had a party. They lived happily ever after.

Khadija Rahman (7)
Greenhill Academy, Glodwick

Upside Down

Their vivid eyes stared into my soul, leaving an aura of terror radiating in the air. I shut my eyes and once I opened them, I found myself running for what seemed forever until I heard guffawing from behind. I checked to look to see nothing but dead ends. I continued running eagerly to find some way out of here. When I saw a tall, dark figure, time stopped. He vanished. And the guffawing started again but this time, villainously louder. I began running but faster. I saw an exit and I saw him but I was too late...

Anabia Kawal (10)
Greenhill Academy, Glodwick

The Possessed iPad

I was on my iPad, looking for ideas for my mini saga. I googled story idea. From the iPad came a crash and a bang. The iPad started shaking, an orange glow came from the screen. I was really scared and didn't know what was going on. Was it a monster coming from another world through my iPad? Or had my iPad been taken over by mini computer gremlins? I started sweating and shaking with fear. What on earth was happening? I plucked up the courage to look at the screen. Silly me, it was just a WhatsApp call.

Maya Choudhury (9)
Greenhill Academy, Glodwick

The Strongest Karate Kid Ever

Once there lived the strongest karate kid ever. His name was Owin, he was a black belt. Owin was so strong he could knock everybody out. The sensei teachers were very impressed with him so they made him a sensei. He got two very special jobs, one was to test people on their grading and to judge people on their competition fighting. When his parents heard about this, they bought Owin a karate DVD, shin pads and foot pads. Owin was so happy because he always dreamt of having them.

Halima Sadia (9)
Greenhill Academy, Glodwick

The Monster Man

In the dark house, a little boy named Joe went into his home and he met his middle-aged mum who had long, blonde hair. She told him to go in the gloomy, dark attic. When he got his heavy box, he heard a creak and a roar! Then he spotted a monster right in front of him, it ate him all up. All was left was his ripped clothes. Then his mum came upstairs, scared what would happen, but she had spotted the monster. So she ran quickly out of the house without looking behind her.

Muhammed Ali
Greenhill Academy, Glodwick

In The Dark Forest

At night-time, five boys were dared to go in the creepy, dark forest. They went deeper and the boys got lost. Suddenly, they heard a loud buzzing sound. The boy screamed and began to run. One of the boys heard a crunch, he kept running and running as fast as he could. He turned around and looked up to see a man who was very tall and scary. He was like death. The man looked in the boy's eyes. The boy's eyes went red but he escaped to find lots of people for help.

Muhammad Yahya Khan (8)
Greenhill Academy, Glodwick

The Stolen Jewels

I was writing in my diary but then I heard a bang. I looked outside and there was an evil pirate trying to open the haunted house where all of the jewels were. It was up to me to save the haunted house. So that night, I got out my sword, quickly got dressed into my adventure clothes and set off. The bad pirate was trying to open the door. As soon as I opened it, I screamed at him then he screamed louder. He screamed so loud. He ran back to his old, dusty city.

Saffa Fatima (8)
Greenhill Academy, Glodwick

Heads Or Tails?

It was all a blur at first, the only thing that remained in my mind was the frantic *thump* in my heart. It all started with me, being so naive and young, entering a cave.

"A dragon's lair?" I had whispered while entering quite an accurate representation of what I would have thought a lair would've looked like. Icy-blue, glazing icicles ordering a sparkling waterfall which cascaded over the lip of the cave, but something wasn't right because I could feel a pair of beady eyes watching me. Then, a chill flew up my spine. I was going to die.

Beatrice Olafusi (10)
Janet Duke Primary School, Laindon

Ocean Girl

Eliza Oceania loved the ocean. She loved the water and the sea animals inside it. She loved the whales, jellyfish and even the stingrays. Every day, she'd go down to the beach and go into the water.

One day, she went down into the water and whistled. She had called all the animals at a command. She was amazed at what she had done. She was the ocean's daughter! Suddenly, something floated down into Eliza's hands. She opened the letter. It was a letter from Hogwarts. It said they wanted her to come to Hogwarts because she had supernatural abilities.

Darcey Elizabeth Wealthall (10)

Janet Duke Primary School, Laindon

Plum Poison

One evening, a former detective told his children a story.

"I was a young lad when I was told to search the body of the richest man in town who had recently been killed. There was no blood on him or any fingerprints nearby. Me and my partner found a pipless plum that had been chewed a little bit. There was no poison around his mouth and in the end, we came to the conclusion that he choked on the plum pip."

Detective Charles kissed his kids' foreheads and his wife entered. She smiled. They were truly happy together.

Katy-Rose Edwards (10)

Janet Duke Primary School, Laindon

Sea Life

I jumped through the tunnel and swam to Sea City. As I arrived, I glanced at starfish, octopuses and seahorses with their families. I was surprised by how Sea City changed. I continued swimming. Afterwards, I saw my house which was stable. Before I went inside my house, I still wanted to observe Sea City. I proceeded to the local sea shops which sold more fashionable clothes than the old times. It was already shadowy as night. As quickly as possible, I returned back home and went to bed. A new day was waiting for me.

Rose Ever Ikpeba (11)

Janet Duke Primary School, Laindon

Death Life

Hi, my name is Rose. I am 89 years old. I feel so weak and it is hard for me to move. I feel like I'm dying. Now, I am in hospital. I know something is wrong. I have now passed away, I am up in heaven. Next minute, I am a skeleton who can move, dance, even run. I feel like I am on Earth again. I have had picnics with my best friends. I have spent time going to the heaven gym. Now it has been a year, I am now finding it hard to move again.

Chloe Tilley (10)
Janet Duke Primary School, Laindon

The Truth About Magic

This story starts hundreds of years ago when the world was full of magic. The world was amazing, no one harmed anyone. Hundreds of years later, a girl called Lily still believed in magical creatures. Everyone at school bullied her but she didn't care. When she got home, she heard her parents saying that she should go to a mental hospital. Lily was furious, she decided to run away. When she was running, her eyes were closed and when she opened them, she was somewhere very far from home. She was in an enchanted forest, with mermaids, unicorns and fairies.

Maisie Grace Midgley (9)
Larkfield Primary School, Southport

The Case Of The Invisible Man

In the dead of night, he struck. Sirens wailed, alarms blasted, lights flashed. In the morning, a guard checked the security cameras but there was nothing! He watched as the vault door swung open by itself and money floated out. So they decided to call a detective, the best in the business, but he couldn't find anything.

As he snooped around the crime scene, a child called out, "Hey, what are those marks in the mud?"

The detective followed them and they came to a house. He opened the door and there was the culprit, a scientist, the invisible man.

Matthew Hand (10)
Larkfield Primary School, Southport

Emit And The Space Travel

Suddenly, as I took my go on the mysterious board game, my head started to feel tingly.

Lewis shouted my name, "Emit!"

I noticed I was disappearing.

"Lewis! Help!"

Ten minutes later, I was in a pitch-black rocky cave. I was all drowsy and dizzy. Scared that I didn't know where I was, I heard a noise. It sounded like a *screech!* I was frightened to death. Shadows started to surround me. Then... run! It was an alien. I just started running without knowing and my knees were tripping over my feet. Then I was back in bed!

Theo Johnson (9)

Larkfield Primary School, Southport

Past Comes To The Present

One day, Lilly was playing in the garden when suddenly, she heard a crash and a bang! Lilly jumped over the short fence and ran over. What she saw was almost unbelievable. This was what she saw. She saw Gorgon Medusa fighting God Hercules. Lilly ran and leapt over a fence. She told her brother, then told him everything. They were two special children because they were son and daughter of the great daughter of Zeus. They used their powers to defeat the snake army but Medusa had disappeared. They looked everywhere but she had gone for now.

Rose Jackson (7)

Larkfield Primary School, Southport

Mysterious Myth

She was just about to leave for a challenging adventure. Adri thought it would be harder than it sounded, and she was right indeed. It took days, weeks, even a few months! Her family got so worried, they thought she might have been hurt or even the 'D' word. Although she was as perfect as a pretty princess, when she finally got to the place she had been looking for, it was beautiful, except for that there was a dragon. It took some time for them to become friends. So then Adri named the dragon, Magic. So they were happy!

Lucy Jolly (8)
Larkfield Primary School, Southport

2019 Lost On An Island

I looked through the window and peered down at a gleaming crystal. Before I went to school, I picked up the crystal and ran to school. Just at that moment, my hip started getting hot. Suddenly, I realised that it was the crystal. Everything froze for a second... Then it was dark, everything was blurry. I started opening my eyes. I pictured a large tree. In the distance, I saw my school friends. I saw no school, no house and no food. We were lost. Larkfield was gone. I was worried. It was 2019, I was lost on an island.

Harriet Smith (9) & Amelia Selby (10)
Larkfield Primary School, Southport

One Big Dream!

One night, a girl called Lucy couldn't get to sleep so she read a book called Under The Sea, and she finally fell asleep. She had this dream about her and her jellyfish teddy going into the book, Under The Sea, that she was reading earlier. In Under The Sea, Lucy turned into a mermaid and her jellyfish teddy, Pinky, came alive! They saw a real dolphin, a blue whale and lots of scaly fish. She and Pinky went deep down in the sea and found a little kingdom. In the kingdom, it was so friendly and fun. They stayed!

Heidi Mabel Sunners (9)
Larkfield Primary School, Southport

A Little Christmas Tree In The Forest

A little Christmas tree in the forest, it wasn't just a little Christmas tree, someone young lived there. Her name was Oceana, she had no money and she was a child. Her parents died in 1922. Then suddenly, an enormous dragon was trying to get the child. So her Aunty May came to rescue her. She was very happy. Oceana ran, didn't care if she fell over, she just kept running. Then her mum's skeleton came, she had a wedding dress which had holes in it. Oceana was very scared and ran away from the creepy, scary dress.

Isabella Huang (7)
Larkfield Primary School, Southport

The Haunted Campsite

Mia and Daniel go into a tent and come out in a haunted campsite, where there's ghosts and spiders. It's always night there but where they usually are, it's day, then night. It's all scary and dark. Then Mia finds a trapdoor in the ground. They go through the trapdoor and get to a room with lots of toys. Daniel says to Mia that he saw a toy move.

Mia then says, "Don't be silly, Daniel, toys don't move."

They go back through the tent and get back to their nice campsite and have a calm, normal day.

Evie Lavery (9)
Larkfield Primary School, Southport

The Land Of Doom!

Crash! Willow woke up. *Crash!* I woke up and Mum was not there... I screamed and the monster under my bed awoke from his deep sleep.

Willow ran into my room and said, "What was that teeth-gnashing noise?"

I shouted, "I have a monster under my bed!"

Willow screamed, "Arghhhhh!"

Rip! Bang! The monster showed himself. He was hairy, brown, terrifying and mean. We ran downstairs and locked the door. Then ran outside and told some village people. They did not believe us apart from one. She said it had happened to them once.

Holly Millward (8)

Park Wood Schools Federation, Rainham

The Fairy Land Mystery

I was playing.
I had just finished playing when someone called, "Come on down!"
I didn't know who said it. It didn't sound like Dad or my brother. I was scared. I didn't want to go down or peek. I thought it was a fairy-napper. I shivered. I heard a *creak!* I didn't know how to act or how I would even speak. I lost my mind, and my marbles. I thought, *how can I go and see what is happening without being seen?* But then someone came into my room, it was Mum all along. I was so relieved.

Grace Burberry (7)
Park Wood Schools Federation, Rainham

The Enchanted Forest

I awoke on my sofa, looking at the enchanted forest. I decided to go exploring. I ran outside into my garden to open the gate. I tiptoed onto the softest grass I had ever felt and remembered I was barefoot. I turned around and the gate had disappeared into thin air. Suddenly, I saw a breathtaking shadow and I remembered what Mum had said. "Do not go into the forest because of the three-headed dog!"
I saw it, it was howling wildly. I reversed and luckily bumped into a woodcutter who shoved away the dog and I thanked him.

Mia Becconsall (8)
Park Wood Schools Federation, Rainham

Creepy Street

I stepped out of the door. I walked out of town into Creepy Street. I saw a freaky ghost, it made me shiver. I nearly fell to the ground.

I quickly ran to something or someone to defeat the ghost. Then I saw something shimmering on the floor. It was words. I read them, they said, 'Happy Halloween?'. I realised the ghost was a fake, a load of children dressed up in Halloween clothes. I saw a shop. I bought some very spooky clothes and played trick or treat with the children. Then I got back in my normal clothes.

Emmie Faith Walker (8)

Park Wood Schools Federation, Rainham

The Land Of Doom!

I was just sitting in my bed when I heard a loud *bang* coming from downstairs. I thought it was a dream but it wasn't... I heard a voice coming from the kitchen.

It said, "Emilia, I'm in the front room."

But I heard it coming from the kitchen. Strange! But nothing was there so I went to do what I was doing in the first place, then I heard the loud bang again.

It said, "I'm next to you."

I screamed then ran away and ever since, they called it The Land of Doom!

Emilia Payne (7)

Park Wood Schools Federation, Rainham

Candy Girl

I made candy in the morning just before Candy School. Anyway, I'm called Candy Girl. I always make candy for breakfast. I normally have candyfloss, it's delicious. My brother is called Candy Boy, he eats more candy than me. I think he is greedy, it is only because Mum buys more candy for him and not me. It's not fair! I had candy all over me because someone came in the door and it came into my room. I didn't know who it was... it was a gooey alien so I slapped it with my teddy! Now, it's gone.

Jessie Gore (7)
Park Wood Schools Federation, Rainham

Sweets And Rainbows

I heard a strange noise but then it went away. So I went back to sleep but then it came back. I got up out of bed and went downstairs. Then in the black darkness of midnight, a shadow came out and it was... a rainbow dancing and singing lollipop! I played, sang and danced with her. Her name was Star. But then a creak came from down below. It was really mysterious and really creepy. I looked down. It was a really cute puppy. So we all played together.
But then I said, "It was all a dream. Phew!"

Savannah Morrison (8)
Park Wood Schools Federation, Rainham

The World Of Darkness!

Finally, I crept out of my territory, not knowing what was going to happen to it. Suddenly, creepy shadows surrounded me. I started to panic, how could I defeat them? I went in my cave for a very long time, wondering where they had come from. Suddenly, I had a plan. I took off the cover of my habitat. Finally, they were gone. I went to my cave but there was another creature. I was stunned. I finally had a friend in my cave. We played together, we had fun together and we played games. I loved playing together.

Ronin (7)

Park Wood Schools Federation, Rainham

The Scare Of Me

I awoke from my dream. The house was normal before I saw a dragon flying round the house. I was so scared, I didn't know what to do. I tried to run but the door was blocked so I hid under the covers. Even worse, nobody was at home. I found a secret base but it was full of monsters, it was dreadful. It was like a haunted house. Then I properly opened my eyes, the monsters were actually... my family! The dragon was a toy aeroplane, but why was an aeroplane near my house hanging from my bedroom ceiling?

Oliver Wood (8)

Park Wood Schools Federation, Rainham

Tyrannosaurus

Once there was an egg, and that egg was a very lucky egg which had survived since the dinosaurs. Then 200 years later, the egg hatched and inside was a snake, well, not just any snake, me! Yes, I am a snake and my name is... erm, I don't really have a name so I'm going to call myself Tyrannosaurus, yes that sounds like a good name. Now when I went through the jungle, I saw a fossil and a fossil scanner. Suddenly, I evolved into a snake with wings, legs and arms. It was very weird.

Ethan Newman (7)

Park Wood Schools Federation, Rainham

The Beach!

I woke up five minutes ago. Suddenly, I realised that I was at the beach. Then I went to the water and found an ancient bottle with a letter in it. Next, I saw a shark furiously coming towards me... As quick as I could, I swam out of the sea but I was stuck so I pulled as hard as I could to safety. Luckily, I just got to safety when the shark was there and just about to demolish me. I relaxed by sunbathing. I made some pizza and I demolished my pizza. It was scrumptious.

Zack Andrew Gibbs (7)
Park Wood Schools Federation, Rainham

The Snowmonster's Attack

I leapt out of my igloo but soon I found the great Snowmonster blocking my way. I grabbed a pole and started to get it out but it just came back in. I fought for days, nights, months and years until I decided it was enough. I scrambled quickly up onto my wardrobe and slowly crawled over to the other side. The monster stared up at me, I dodged his eyes. I sighed and clicked the power switch. Oh no! That was the lights. I scrambled to the heating and watched him melt.

Freya Hatton (7)

Park Wood Schools Federation, Rainham

The Washout!

When I woke up this morning, my mum called me down for breakfast. It was a sunny day outside, so me and my friends decided to go to the beach. When me, my mum and my friends got there, we decided to go in the water a little bit. When we got to the sea, there was a big wave and it toppled over us. No one else could get out of the waves. Thankfully, we had breathing equipment on so we saved everyone. I wanted to go home so we could sit on my bed and watch a movie.

Molly Swanson Kirwan (7)
Park Wood Schools Federation, Rainham

Pup Rescue

I woke at seven in the morning. I asked my mum if I could go out and she said okay. So I went to my horse's stable and went to round up my huskies. When I had all my huskies, I realised one of the pups was missing... I dashed down the stairs and realised the front door was wide open. I heard a creak on the floorboard and it was heading straight towards me. I ran straight out of the front door and slammed it. Finally, I found the pup, its fur was freezing.

Libby Paternoster (7)
Park Wood Schools Federation, Rainham

The Haunted House

I woke up holding a flashlight and heard a *creak!* I ran and I heard a huge lightning strike. I saw a ghost and ran. He had black eyes and a white body. It was creepy. As he walked, I heard another *creak!* I got down the stairs and I was puzzled. The ghost fell to the floor like a white sheet. I looked, I saw a trapdoor. I opened it up and another ghost was in there. I was puzzled. I didn't know what to do. I saw it was my mum and dad.

Jack Paul Tandy (8)
Park Wood Schools Federation, Rainham

The Land Of Doom

I found myself in a village called the Land of Doom!
I was with my brother called Jake. The Land of
Doom was very sad, poor and hungry. But Jake
and I were happy, calm and had a bit of money.
Our mum was a bit of a drama queen and our dad
was very emotional too.

We went for a walk and an old man came up to us
and said, "What are you doing alone?" in an old
voice.

Suddenly, we were both gone! The old man looked
around for us. Gone!

Grace Bevis (8)
Park Wood Schools Federation, Rainham

The Haunted Ship

I had some toast in the morning until my mum said we were going to the beach. When we went to the beach, we had a little paddle in the shallow water until a huge tidal wave came along. Suddenly, we were washed away into the sea, but luckily, I found a boat. I went to where the driver was but he wasn't there. That meant the boat was sinking... I had to get off but now the door was locked. I had to drive to safety. But the boat wouldn't start...

Harrison Pope (7)

Park Wood Schools Federation, Rainham

Candy City

Once there was a girl who loved candy but one day, she was asleep when she dreamt of Candy City. But it was real and it was a beautiful place of candy. She knocked on the door and a girl answered. Then she saw a giant butterfly made out of cotton candy, but it nearly ate her.

She wanted to go home but then the girl said, "If you meet my mum, she will give you a wish so you can go home."

Then I realised it was just a dream.

Myah Flemming (7)
Park Wood Schools Federation, Rainham

Creepy Woods

I woke up. I went through the Door of Doom. It was pitch-black. Rain dropped. It made me scream. So I stuck up a piece of paper in it. But there was a person that gave me a blanket. It was my mum. I went somewhere and I was there for a year. I missed home but I met a skeleton. It screamed at me. I screamed back. He picked me up and took me in a creepy woods. I lifted up his head and it was a fake. The sun was up. I was happy. Yay!

Selyena Sekmen (7)
Park Wood Schools Federation, Rainham

The Adventure Of The Stingrays!

I loved to save the stingrays and feed them but then everybody made fun of me. So I thought I should stop saving the stingrays and quit. Then everybody didn't make fun of me and I was happy but sad at the same time because I loved saving the stingrays. However, my mum was mad at me! But then I wanted to do it more than ever. So I did but was worried that my friends might make fun of me again but they didn't. I was so happy again!

Isla-Rose Vernon (8)

Park Wood Schools Federation, Rainham

At Home

I woke up at nine o'clock and put my slippers on and went downstairs. I went and got changed. Then I went to my mum, I said to her, "Can I play with my friends?"
She said, "Okay."
So I went and played with both of my friends. When we were playing, I saw a stranger. He took us and then we started to cry. Ivy and Pippa were so naughty that he left us on the way. We walked home to my house.

Brooke Lenihan (8)
Park Wood Schools Federation, Rainham

The Land Of Doom

Andy and I were just sitting in our bed when we fell to sleep and suddenly, we fell to sleep and went in this mysterious dream. We were in this weird land that was dingy and dark, so we thought to hide in the bushes. Suddenly, we heard weird noises, we didn't know what it was. We were so frightened, we wanted our mums.

Then we woke up and heard someone say, "I know you and this is the Land of Doom!"

Heidi Ongley (8)

Park Wood Schools Federation, Rainham

The Land Of Doom

I went to my new home. As I saw next door, I saw a nutcracker. I went to the gate and it moved! I called Mum but she wasn't there, neither was my dad. As the rain began, the nutcracker was right near me! I went to my house in a frenzy. I got a knife and chopped it. But in eight seconds, it was fixed. I ran down the street. I got to Park Lane, no one was there. I just recognised it was a dream.

Finley Bunting (7)
Park Wood Schools Federation, Rainham

Lost Jungle

I had finished saving the jungle. Then I found myself lost. Suddenly, I fell into a huge pond of alligators but someone saved me and put me on land. I woke up and looked for the one who saved me.

A voice said, "Hello and welcome. I guess you're lost. Let me take you, it's straight ahead."

So I went to my car, then I saw my mum.

Thomas Harrison-Brookes (8)

Park Wood Schools Federation, Rainham

Oh No!

One day, me and my friends, Layla, April and Lexi, were in the forest. Suddenly, we heard a strange noise in the distance.

"What was that?" repetitively asked April.

We crept closer and closer towards the strange sound. It was a massive, erupting, funny-looking volcano. I saw something yelping, it looked scared and lonely. I just knew we had to get it out. We slowly crept towards the erupting volcano, we were white as a sheet. It was a fluffy, pink unicorn. I climbed upon the volcano and pulled it out. Hopefully, it wouldn't happen again.

April Charmaine Freeman (10), Lemie Francis (11) & Layla

Pelsall Village School, Pelsall

Finally

One day, there was a lost, lonely, scared unicorn that was lost in a gloomy dark forest, she wondered where her parents had gone. She yelped to try and give a signal to her parents, her name was Lucy. She trotted down a steep hill and tripped on a stone, her horn snapped off in an instance.

When a day passed, she had finally found her parents, they went to hug each other when suddenly a siren went off, she was so scared that she went to hide and her mother followed her they were both very scared.

Lemie Francis (10)
Pelsall Village School, Pelsall

A Letter From Hogwarts

Suddenly, I saw a penguin, he had a unicorn horn, coming towards me. My heart stopped. It was a letter from Hogwarts! It flew through my bedroom window. By the way, my name is Amy. It sat on my bed. He had a nametag on, his name was Snow. I was in Gryffindor. I already had all the stuff I needed for school, now all I needed to do was get there. Thirty minutes later, I was lost. It all looked the same. Surprisingly, I saw something flying, it was Snow. Thankfully, he knew the way. Snow rescued me.

Lilli-Mai Smith (10)
Pelsall Village School, Pelsall

The Land Of Unicorns

I turned around and saw the mysterious door that had appeared in my bedroom wall just a few minutes ago. My gaze turned towards the scene in front of me. Unicorns scattered into my view, as my mouth dropped open. Never in my life had I believed in unicorns, so I was now in total shock! My mind filled with questions. Why had this happened to me? Was I dreaming or not? Was I the only one that this had happened to? I had no idea what the answers were, but I knew that my adventure had only just begun!

Bethlyn Rose Brotherton (11)
Pelsall Village School, Pelsall

The Case At 10 Downing Street

I had just received an email from the Prime Minister's security, Jim Brody, saying 'you need to come to 10 Downing Street because the Prime Minister has been kidnapped'!

"Oh my!" I gasped.

Well, it's a job for Detective Doodle and his detective doggy Barney.

"How do we get there?"

I thought for a while.

"Eureka! That's it!"

In the dead of night, I sneaked onto a cargo train, my dog in my backpack. I got off at London and walked to 10 Downing Street. I knocked on the door, Rex Scar opened the door...

Sonny Lindley (10)

Stella Maris School, Heaton Mersey

The Roman Army Against The Germans

One day the Romans were going into battle against the Germans. The Romans killed thousands but the German leader was strong. The Romans were organised, but the Germans were fast. But it went wrong because one of the Germans accidentally killed their leader and they lost the battle. It was definitely a good win for the Romans. But it was all a trap. When they drank the victory drink to celebrate, they all fell dead! It was poison! Then a new army came with Julius Caesar. "All hail Caesar!" the Romans cried. "We'll give you a parade in Rome."

Bradley Beckford

Stella Maris School, Heaton Mersey

Collision

Bob always dreamed of finding a new planet system and his day had finally arrived. Bob was looking through his telescope when he spotted a strange shape in the Crux Zone near the end of our galaxy. There were two starlight objects orbiting around each other. Bob figured out they were stars on a collision course that looked like it was happening next week, according to Bob's calculations. These stars were too powerful and if they collided it could cause chaos! Bob figured out the best way the fix this was to tell the government, which pretty much sorted it.

Lily (8)

Stella Maris School, Heaton Mersey

Miffy And The Snowman

One night Miffy was sleepwalking, looking for his missing teddy. Then, he walked into his cupboard, woke up and found he was in a freezing cold, snowy forest. He was lonely so he decided to make a snowman. Just then he felt a large bulgy thing in his pocket! It was a carrot! It magically floated onto the snowman's face, as well as coal for feet, eyes and buttons, twigs for arms and a top hat. Suddenly, the snowman came alive and Miffy told him about his missing teddy. They went off together into the distance to find Miffy's missing marvellous teddy.

Agatha Charlotte Hayes (9)

Stella Maris School, Heaton Mersey

Osi And The Mermaid

The day finally came, I could meet the mermaid. I mean I could marry her. Well... yeah! I came to the ocean.

I giggled, "Sass, spread my wings! Yeah!"

I turned into a merman and dived into the ocean. I saw the mermaid!

"Hello there. I can't believe I finally get to meet you." My house is near to the ocean so I said, "Let's go!"

But the mermaid said, "I've got no legs!"

So I giggled, "Sass, give her two amazing legs! Yeah!"

We had a fun time in my cottage playing games! Yeah!

Osikhena Otu (10)

Stella Maris School, Heaton Mersey

Future War

I stepped into the mysterious portal, knowing that I would be taken to a different dimension. When I arrived I noticed that I was in the war, I could smell dusty and horrible air. Suddenly a bullet came across me like it was going 400 miles per hour! Now I was scared to death. As quick as a flash I ran for my life, dodging the bullets and lasers. Just then someone pulled me in.

"Hey! What in the world are you doing?" he said.

"Running for my life and what year is it?" I shouted.

"It's the year 20,000!"

Zak Shahid (10)

Stella Maris School, Heaton Mersey

Knock At The Door

There was a knock on the door: it was 3am in the morning. There was another knock, but when I opened the door there was nobody there! I waited an hour... But nobody came. So I went back to sleep. When I awoke, I heard footsteps downstairs. "Hello!" I shouted, confused, but got no response. I got out of my bed, had a shower, got dressed, had breakfast, brushed my teeth and watched TV for an hour. Then I heard the footsteps again, so I went into the hall and found my friend just sitting there, smiling creepily...

Max Edgar (8)
Stella Maris School, Heaton Mersey

Another Exhausting Day

Another day catching crime and I was exhausted. I went home to my base and sat down in a comfy chair! I needed to work out who was the master thief behind all this trouble. Eventually, I figured out who it was so I went outside to locate him. I used my laser eyes to see through buildings then I saw him hiding in this underground lair stroking a white cat. I used my super-breath to blow him into jail.

Everyone was outside and watching on TV and they cheered and shouted, "Well done, Supergirl! You saved the world!"

Zoha Mahmood (8)

Stella Maris School, Heaton Mersey

The Derelict House

One foggy night, I was playing with my dog. He was starting to act very funny and uncomfortable. Suddenly, my dog started walking into the front garden and onto the road. I followed him and he led me into the graveyard!
"Why did you lead me here?" I asked.
The dog barked at a derelict house. I hesitated, but then I opened the half-broken door and stood staring at a tight hallway with a door at the end. Slowly I walked through the door and there I saw a clown: smiling!
"No! Please! Help!"

Oscar Hargreaves

Stella Maris School, Heaton Mersey

World War 10

I'd just got through the time portal and there seemed to be a war.

A man called, "It's World War 10! Do you want to be in the action?"

I replied, "Yes! Wait! Why are there robots and aliens here?"

He shouted, "They've taken over! It's men versus aliens and robots."

I found their base, there were no guards. I found the ultimate taser and put it in my pocket. Just then, robots grabbed me and threw me in jail. I had an escape plan but there was no power in the taser! I'm stuck in this tiny jail!

William Taylor (8)
Stella Maris School, Heaton Mersey

Snake Woman's New Side

One day there was a villain called Snake Woman and she suddenly found a stone. It was saying, "Join me on the dark side!"

Snake Woman replied, "Of course, Master!"

Suddenly, the stone told her, "Find a snake and rip it in half and you will find a tracking device and that will show you where I am, and show me where you are and I have some people that will find you with a snap of my fingers! Then I'll show you the way."

"I will come and find you master and will do everything you say!" she answered.

Lily Richardson-Gormley (8)

Stella Maris School, Heaton Mersey

The Villain Who Pretended To Be A Superhero!

Hello! I'm Evil Tiffany and I'm going to take over the world! My friend, Sonic Selina is, right at this moment, throwing fireballs at Paris! Everyone is crying out for a hero! That's where I come in! I'm going to have to put on a disguise and then I will stand in front of the Eiffel Tower and deflect the fireballs into space! Then I'm going to go into the Superhero Base and send them all on a mission on another planet. While they're gone, I'll take over the world! Mwhahaha!

Rose Ameerah Khan (8)

Stella Maris School, Heaton Mersey

The Tomb

I was finally back in Egypt on an adventure. I'd been here once before when I lost my cat. I had heard of a mummy's tomb nearby, but I had to hurry or a grave robber might get in before me. I was almost at my destination when I heard a meow from a pyramid. I touched the bricks and a door opened. It was filled with precious gold and shining silver. I saw a tiny heart-shaped coffin. I opened it, there was a small mummy inside. I unwrapped it and it was my cat and underneath her were jewels!

Megan Carter-Jones
Stella Maris School, Heaton Mersey

The Letter From Hogwarts

I was in Hogwarts and Professor McGonagall was writing a letter. I wondered who she was writing to. I sneakily went to see but I couldn't see a word. She posted the magic letter. It should have gone to Dumbledore but it went to a ghost! McGonagall got everyone because it wasn't safe. When the ghost came and Professor McGonagall tried to protect us, I was so scared. I felt I was going to be sick. The ghost had a chunk taken out of it and beastly eyes. Oh no! What was going to happen?

Cara Taylor
Stella Maris School, Heaton Mersey

The Ghost

One day I was in my house eating dinner. Suddenly the lights went off! What was that? It was the generator. Phew! Five minutes later, it happened again. I asked my Mum to check the generator because it kept going on and off!
"Mum, I am going back to sleep."
When I lay in bed, it happened again. What was that? I woke up and I was in shock. I saw a white cloth flying. I got up quickly and went to the cloth and pulled it. Behind it was my big brother, Roderick!

Hadi Ejaz (11)
Stella Maris School, Heaton Mersey

A New Kind Of Library

As I put my hand on to the dusty old library book, wondering what it was called, I got totally sucked inside and then total darkness! When I woke up, I first thought that this world was the same as my own. That was until a ghost swam straight through me! I screamed in terror and when I finally calmed down, I looked around in horror and saw a gruesome pumpkin face laughing at me and I heard zombies groaning! It was then that I realised that this was the land of Halloween! Noooo!

Eva Cunningham (8)
Stella Maris School, Heaton Mersey

The Mysterious Night

I woke up to a bang! I saw bright lights from the forest, I raced outside to take a closer look. I made my way towards the light. It was so cold I felt I had frostbite. I had mixed feelings: scared yet curious at the same time. Suddenly a smiling face peered at me! It started to run laps around me like a puppy. I held out my hand, he followed me home. I gave it a homemade hot water bottle and my dog's old bed. Next morning the hot water bottle was there but the bed was empty!

Lily-Mae Bullas (9)
Stella Maris School, Heaton Mersey

The Curious Mountain

As I walked on a strange mountain I saw a stunning red light. It was a gem glistening! When I held it up, it glowed gold and I faded into dust! Next, I was in a tomb, I saw a door but as I opened it, sand was filling the tomb. I ran to the door but it was locked! The sand got to my chest and a small door above me opened up! Now the sand was up to my neck! With a little courage, I grabbed on the side and pulled myself to the outside and safety!

Eason Fong (10)
Stella Maris School, Heaton Mersey

YOUNG WRITERS
INFORMATION

We hope you have enjoyed reading this book – and that you will continue to in the coming years.

If you're a young writer who enjoys reading and creative writing, or the parent of an enthusiastic poet or story writer, do visit our website **www.youngwriters.co.uk**. Here you will find free competitions, workshops and games, as well as recommended reads, a poetry glossary and our blog. There's lots to keep budding writers motivated to write!

If you would like to order further copies of this book, or any of our other titles, then please give us a call or order via your online account.

Young Writers
Remus House
Coltsfoot Drive
Peterborough
PE2 9BF
(01733) 890066
info@youngwriters.co.uk

Join in the conversation!
Tips, news, giveaways and much more!

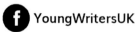 **YoungWritersUK**    **@YoungWritersCW**